WAY OF THE ODYSSEY SHORT STORY COLLECTION VOLUME 3

CONNOR WHITELEY

No part of this book may be reproduced in any form or by any electronic or mechanical means. Including information storage, and retrieval systems, without written permission from the author except for the use of brief quotations in a book review.

This book is NOT legal, professional, medical, financial or any type of official advice.

Any questions about the book, rights licensing, or to contact the author, please email connorwhiteley@connorwhiteley.net

Copyright © 2024 CONNOR WHITELEY

All rights reserved.

DEDICATION
Thank you to all my readers without you I couldn't do what I love.

CREATING ITHANE

This single event changed the galaxy forever and had the power to doom, save or kill all life.

When people normally say they used to be great, be something or even remotely important, they're lying. They really are. When I was in the Imperial Army fighting on a particularly hard world to pronounce (not that it matters now that it's a lifeless husk), I knew a man that claimed to be a billionaire, the best friend of the glorious Rex and even an inventor.

After spending three years with him in infected mud trenches fighting an enemy he couldn't even understand, I quickly realised that he was a liar, a nobody, a person who was useless and always doomed to die.

You see my name is Ianthe Veilwalker. I don't know why my surname is so weird and futuristic but it works and my parents loved me even as the laser blasts from their Imperial Masters cooked their brains alive. And I did have a good childhood and even when I was serving the Rex in the army I always fought to protect humanity.

That's how I ended up here.

I sat in one of the two corners of my black crystal prison cell that was barely tall enough for me to stand up in. It wasn't wide enough for me to do three steps in any direction and my legs were hardly short.

The entire prison cell was tiny and stunk of blood, corruption and charred flesh so I knew I wasn't the first human to be trapped here.

I had to admit that I really did like the small black crystal dome at the very top of my cell. I didn't doubt for a moment it was what my alien captors were using to watch me. The Dark Keres, the foul humanoid alien race that wanted to resurrect their God of Death, always liked to watch me.

I sort of got the sense that they feared me for some reason and they wanted me dead at all cost, and yet they hadn't tried to kill me just yet. It was weird and strange and I was glad they were next to useless at trying to kill me.

But today felt different.

It wasn't the normal hum, pop and vibration of the air that I now understood to be the life-saving magic that kept the Dark Keres and myself alive. But I felt like someone or something else was watching me and focusing on me like I was about to be picked for something I didn't understand.

Granted I could have just been going mad in this tiny damn prison cell, but that was how the Dark Keres won their psychological wars without even lifting up one of their magical fingers.

You see I had just decided that the Rex was a complete and utter dickhead that only cared about himself and corruption so I went rogue. Me and my squad mates decided to go wrong but the Dark Keres attacked us in our white pod-like shuttle.

We all tried to fight as much as we could but it was useless. The Dark Keres ambushed us and there was nothing we could even remotely do to save ourselves.

I was the only survivor and that was how I ended up in a damn prison cell waiting to die a death that I hoped would come soon. I love humanity, I love life and I want to protect humanity no matter the cost but being in a prison cell just isn't how I want to live.

Someone laughed behind me.

I stood up and noticed how one of the dark crystal walls that trapped me had turned see-through. I stared at the foul, awful Dark Keres with their almost translucent skin, humanoid features and burnt red veins that made him look like a demon.

He smiled at me but I could tell there was no warmth, interest or concern behind those eyes. There was only a lust for murder and pain and my death.

I instantly knew that it was my time to die but knowing the Keres they were certainly not going to make it boring at all.

As the Dark Keres clicked his fingers I felt a fog come over my mind and I collapsed to the ground as my world turned black.

Little did Ianthe know that on the other side of the galaxy a ritual was happening that would change her life and the fate of the galaxy forever.

***

I woke a few moments later and frowned as I found myself in the middle of a massive Colosseum made from the same awful black crystal as my prison cell. It was perfectly smooth, glassy and I just wanted to smash it up, ideally with the skull of a Dark Keres but all I could focus on was the strange ambition of escape.

The Colosseum was immense and I tried to focus on the thousands upon thousands of Dark Keres with their pale skin, awful humanoid features and deranged looks as they focused on me. But I could feel their dark magical energy crackling in the air.

I covered my nose as the air was filled with the horrid aroma of charred flesh, burnt ozone and another more alien smell that I really didn't want to identify.

I had always known that the Dark Keres loved playing games in their Colosseums, and this warband had to be powerful in their hierarchy if they had a Colosseum, but I could feel fear in the air too.

I flat out did not understand how I was now feeling things because this made no sense. I was a normal human woman that wanted to protect, treasure and love life but this ability to actually sense things was just weird.

"See what is about you woman," someone said in a deranged voice.

I shook my head as three human corpses appeared around me that hadn't been there moments ago. They were all former soldiers like me and they had been completely stripped of armour, weapons and skin as their corpses laid there.

At least I now knew how the Dark Keres dealt with their criminals. They simply killed them in the Colosseums, and the bastards used this for sport and entertainment too. They really were monsters.

"Let us give the Dark Lord Geneitor," someone said, "a game to remember,"

I instantly broke out into a fighting position as I felt the ground vibrate and then a very tall Dark Keres woman appeared. Her white skin glowed dark and magical energy crackled around her.

She had to be a Keres witch corrupted by their God Geneitor to be a mindless instrument of his will.

I so badly wished I had a weapon.

The woman shot out her hands.

Black torrents of fire rushed towards me.

I rolled to one side.

The fire chased me.

The fire turned into dogs.

The dogs chased me.

I ran.

I couldn't allow the fire to touch me.

The witch unleashed more fire.

More dogs formed.

Twenty dogs chased me.

I spun around.

I had to fight death with life.

I charged.

The dogs hesitated.

I didn't.

I leapt into the air.

Kicking a fiery dog in the head.

It died.

Agony shot through my leg.

The dogs charged at me.

I punched them.

Kicked them.

Snapped their bones.

My skin burnt.

My clothes fused to my skin.

The witch made a black fiery sword form in her hand.

She flew at me.

She swung.

Again.

And again.

I ducked.

I rolled.

I fled.

Black magical energy gripped a hold of me.

Throwing me towards her.

I flew towards the witch.

She raised her sword. I grabbed it as I slammed into her.

I thrusted it into her. The witch died.

As soon as the witch's corpse disappeared, the entire damn Colosseum went deadly silent and they all looked to a particular point that I couldn't see. Maybe they wanted to ask their warlord what was going to happen next. Maybe they might give me my freedom.

I seriously doubted it.

"Most impressive human," someone said, "but let us see how you do against the most devout servants of Geneitor,"

I shook my head. "All I want is to live. Protect life. Save people. That is all I want so I don't want to kill you,"

I didn't know why I said that but it just felt right in the moment. But as a massive wolf the size of a shuttle appeared at the other end of the Colosseum I seriously knew that I could never ever reason with the Dark Keres.

The wolf charged.

I went to roll.

I felt a sword at my feet. The same one the witch had used. I grabbed it.

I charged at the wolf.

The wolf charged even faster.

I jumped into the air.

I swung the sword.

The sword shattered as it touched the wolf.

The Dark Keres laughed.

It was deafening.

The wolf chomped down on my leg.

Throwing me about like a rag doll. Breaking my leg. Shattering bone.

The wolf threw me to one side.

I landed with a thud.

I forced myself up. I couldn't use a leg.

The wolf charged.

I tried to run.

I couldn't.

The wolf whacked me to one side.

I smashed into the black crystal.

The wolf roared.

It was playing with me as it slowly came over to me and I realised that I was going to die here. I was going to become just another victim one of the Dark Keres and my soul or whatever it was called would be tortured and devoured by Geneitor, forever.

It was weird because all I wanted to do was protect people, preserve life and make sure that no one ever harmed an innocent person again.

I stared in utter defiance as the wolf came over to me and grinned with an unnaturally human smile as its fangs got closer.

The wolf snapped me in two.

Everyone cheered, laughed and sang happy songs as the life drained from me but I realised that as everything turned white, that I wasn't actually dead yet.

I saw an immense picture of a Keres woman formed but this woman was kind, angelic and I could feel her sheer aura of life, hope and protection. She was inspiring as hell even though I didn't know her and all she made me want to do was get back to my body and defeat the Dark Keres.

"How badly do you want to protect life human?" the woman asked in perfect Imperial tongue.

"With all my being,"

"Will you serve me and become the Daughter of Genetrix?" the woman asked.

I didn't know what she meant but I knew that Genetrix was the Keres Goddess of life, protection and hope. And if Geneitor was real then she had to be real too.

"Definitely," I said with such rage that I hope she knew how angry I was at the Dark Keres for daring to kill me.

"Then return to life Daughter of Genetrix and free me,"

Before I could ask what she meant I felt pure magical energy pour into me and I was flat out amazed at all the Keres knowledge, forbidden texts and divine guidance that was entering my mind. I might not have known everything about the Keres and their gods but that didn't matter for now.

I opened my eyes back in the Colosseum and I

shook my head at the Wolf.

Everyone noticed what was happening as they stopped their cheering, singing and laughing. And let me tell you hearing that deafening noise stop was shocking as hell.

I thrusted out my hand and an immense white lightning bolt shot out that killed the wolf so quickly that I had to double-check that it had actually died.

"What is this?" everyone shouted.

I smiled as I felt the love, guidance and protection of Genetrix flow through my veins. "This is the future Dark Keres. Genetrix has touched my soul, given me power and now I will make sure you fail to resurrect Geneitor and wipe out all life in the galaxy,"

"Impossible," someone said. "Geneitor is all-powerful. He has a cult dedicated to him and we will find all the Soulstones needed to bring him down,"

"You might have a head start on us. You might have the resources that we don't. But I am the Daughter and Chosen of Genetrix and I will not allow you to live any longer,"

"Kill her lads,"

I just grinned as the stupid Dark Keres leapt down over the Colosseum's black crystal railings as they charged towards me. I flicked my wrists and two huge white swords formed in my hands. And I was so glad I had specialised in sword combat back in the Imperial Army.

I charged.

I swung.

I sliced.

I diced.

It was a slaughter.

I ripped into the flesh of the enemy.

Throats were slashed.

Chests exploded.

Dark Keres screamed out in agony.

There were too many. Too many Dark Keres for me to kill. They would overwhelm me in short order.

I fell back.

I sensed the Keres were behind me.

I ducked. A sword passed behind me.

I realised I had to keep killing. Keep fighting. Keep living.

I didn't know how I knew. But each death brought me closer to my salvation because Genetrix would help me.

Yet first she needed death to power her creation.

I screamed in rage.

I dived forward.

Swinging my swords.

Slashing throats in bloody arcs.

Ramming my swords into chests.

Unleashing torrents of fire with my mind.

A sword slashed my back.

I froze.

The Dark Keres sliced my arms.

I dropped my swords.

The Keres kicked me to the ground.

They jumped on my head.

I screamed in crippling pain.

I unleashed a fireball.

Killing two Keres.

And that was when it happened.

I felt the veil between this reality and the next become paper thin and then they disappeared.

"Come to me Vita," I said.

An immense deafening roar, scream and shout in a language I didn't know all rolled into one echoed across the planet as a blinding white light appeared above me.

Vita was a demon, a demi-God, a creation by divine power that I could summon and I was more than glad about that.

She was a huge Keres woman with golden magical energy crackling around her.

She screamed out. She launched torrents of white fire. She unleashed all her divine power.

The Dark Keres didn't stand a chance as Vita slaughtered them. The Keres tried to run, tried to flee, tried to scream. It didn't matter as Vita cooked them alive, slaughtered them and scooped up their souls so Genetrix could protect them against the predations of Geneitor.

Within a few moments the slaughter was over and Vita just smiled at me, and I wasn't sure if this was Vita smiling or Genetrix. Maybe she was impressed with what I had done, maybe she was pleased to see her Will made real for a change or maybe she was happy that there was now hope in the galaxy that Geneitor and the Dark Keres might not win after all.

I didn't know what had caused this at all. I didn't know why Genetrix had decided on me as the perfect human or living creature for that now, to become part of her. But I didn't care because for the first time in my life, I actually felt like I had a purpose.

I had always been interested and dedicated to protecting, saving and helping to preserve life and now with Genetrix's power I had the ability to do it. So I bowed to Vita as she disappeared and then it was just me left in the darkness of a former Dark Keres world.

But there was a single rose that grew out of the ground, and that really did make me smile. It showed that even in the most deadly of places, life could and would endure and considering the thousands of Imperial worlds that had been rendered lifeless husks by the Rex's pointless wars, that gave me a hell of a lot of hope for the future.

A future I might not have been certain about, but a future I was really, really excited about because I was Ianthe Veilwalker, human and Daughter of Genetrix.

It was my job to stop the Dark Keres from resurrecting Geneitor no matter the cost.

And that meant the entire galaxy depended on

me.

RITUAL OF REBIRTH

After fighting to protect humanity on hundreds of worlds, after killing more enemies than he cared to remember and after being betrayed by more people than he wanted to think about, Commander Jerico Nelson had never ever expected to be in the employ of the very alien race that he had unfortunately killed out of blind obedience to humanity's monstrous leader known as the Rex.

Jerico wasn't particularly a fan of this strategic position as he stood on the very edge of a massive blood-red crater with gentle slopes. The slopes alone with its near perfectly smooth red rocks made this a bad position to defend. Ideally he would have loved to be in a crater with steep slopes that would slow down the enemies. Yet these awful red slopes wouldn't do anything to make his defence job any easier.

The entire red, sandy, rocky planet wasn't ideal for defence. Jerico wasn't a fan of the massive red mountains in the distance that rose up from the ground like daggers, just waiting to kill him, his men and his alien allies.

He really loved positions that were surrounded by flat ground so he could see his enemies for miles before they actually got within striking distance. But he couldn't help his stomach tighten at the very notion of snipers setting up in the mountains to take him and his men out.

The only major benefit of this crater that was there was a small rocky platform that his alien allies, the Keres, had created for him and his men. At least that way if there was an attack then they could easily hide, jump down and use it as their own snipers' nest.

But Jerico just couldn't help focusing on the stormy sky above them. The blood-red clouds with small amounts of crimson swirled in them really didn't make Jerico feel at ease. The gathering storm looked evil, cold and like it was going to be the death of all of them.

The entire planet smelt of damp sand with the odd hint of gun oil, burnt ozone and charred sage from the ritual that the Keres were hoping to perform in the crater. That made the great taste of roast dinner form on his tongue.

Jerico stepped down onto the rocky platform where the five remaining squad mates of his were all playing cards in their black battle armour. They were smiling, having fun and acting like there wasn't a single danger in the galaxy.

Granted Jerico didn't know if the ritual was going to be attacked. He was simply wanting to be sure because the Keres, or as this cult preferred to be called the Daughter of Genetrix, were paying a lot of Rexes for the job.

He still didn't understand how none of the Keres fractions had any sort of currency and their society was based on need and mutual respect. But these Keres were nice, kind and helpful so Jerico didn't mind not understanding everything about them.

Jerico looked down at the bottom of the crater and just shook his head. The Keres were wearing some kind of strange bright white robe that made them look even more like elves and fairies, because of their pointy features, unnaturally thin humanoid body and their almond-shaped eyes.

They had to be finishing up the preparations because Jerico noticed there were the five red, blue and purple Soul stones that the Keres had been obsessed with for months. Apparently each of the Soul Stones contained a Demi-god belonging to their Goddess of Life Genetrix.

Jerico didn't buy it.

But the Rexes were good and he really wanted to upgrade his equipment and actually pay his men so he really, really didn't care.

"Commander we are ready," a Keres said in a scarily good impression of Imperial Tongue.

Jerico nodded and he tightened his grip on his machine gun and he gestured that his men should also start to get ready, because if an attack was going to happen then it was going to happen very, very soon.

Jerico watched his men go up to the top of the ridge of the crater and he was about to join them when he caught what was happening with the Keres below.

All of them were holding hands and sitting on the icy cold floor with sharp shards of rock digging into their asses. The five Soul stones were in the middle and they were glowing.

The Keres started singing a beautifully sweet perfect melody that made Jerico want to cry, something he hadn't done in decades and he felt the air crackle, buzz and hum with magical energy around him.

Jerico looked up and frowned as the thunder roared overhead. The violent storm clouds were coming together and Jerico had a very, very bad feeling about this.

It got even worse when an immense spherical warship belonging to the Rex appeared in-between flashes of lightning.

The Imperium was here and they were going to attack.

Jerico went to shout to the Keres but his mouth was frozen and he felt like something was influencing him not to interfere under any circumstances. And for some reason he obeyed.

He rushed up to the top with the rest of his men.

"We have company," Jerico said.

He nodded at Thomas as he checked his pistols and young Allen looked unsure about his third battle but Jerico had faith in all of his men.

A deafening roar screamed overhead as a nuclear bomb was dropped.

Jerico wanted to scream like the rest of his men but he knew they would be okay for now. The Goddess Genetrix would protect them and as soon as the nuclear bomb touched the top of an invisible dome the sheer extreme impact was reflected.

Jerico's mouth dropped as he saw the sheer destructive power of the bomb rip the Imperial vessel limb from limb.

A Keres screamed in agony.

The storm clouds smashed into each other.

The thunder roared.

It screamed.

It screamed bloody murder.

Jerico's ears started to bleed.

Black lightning shot down around them.

Jerico jumped to one side.

The ritual was starting now and Jerico knew that it flat out couldn't be undone. Something was happening not in this reality but Jerico understood in a way he didn't understand that his life was about to change forever.

A furious roar echoed around the planet as Jerico

saw two white pod-like shuttles were flying towards them. Some damn humans from the Imperial ship had survived.

Jerico clocked that the two shuttles were splitting up.

Jerico grabbed Thomas and Allen and he took them to the other side of the crater.

The shuttle landed with a crash and Jerico aimed his gun at the door of the pod-like shuttle. He wanted, needed to kill these humans to protect whatever was going on.

The shuttle doors exploded open.

The Imperial army soldiers exploded out.

Firing as they went.

Jerico fired back.

Bullets slammed into Jerico's armour.

He stood firm. He couldn't be defeated.

He fired controlled shots.

Bullets screamed through the air.

Smashing into the enemy's faces.

Heads exploded.

Skulls shattered.

Thomas's head imploded.

Jerico ran backwards.

More high-velocity shots screamed at him.

Jerico spun around.

There were snipers in the mountains.

Jerico ran over the ridge of the crater with Allen.

They charged at the soldiers.

Cutting them down.

Jerico unleashed the full power of his gun.

He slaughtered the enemy.

The shuttle exploded.

Throwing them forward.

Jerico slowly forced himself up and he was so glad that he was okay. All the enemies in the shuttle were dead and that him and Allen could now go and reinforce the other position but the storm screamed in terror overhead.

Jerico looked over to Allen's unmoving body and he went over to it. Allen's eyes were glassy and cold and lifeless as Jerico noticed all the metal shards from the shuttle covered his body.

The storm roared overhead.

The wind was howling all around him creating immense sandstorms.

Jerico could barely see where he was going so he allowed his instincts to guide him.

He made his way round the crater but he was annoyed as hell he could no longer hear the gunshots and screaming of the Imperial soldiers. He really hoped that his men were okay.

He couldn't lose them. They had to live. Just had to.

Jerico found his way to the other side and he frowned at the three remaining dead bodies of his men. The other Imperial shuttle had exploded and the mountain in the distance shattered as a lightning bolt from the storm smashed into it.

"Help Genetrix!" a Keres shouted at the top of her lungs.

The storm grew even more intense.

Jerico ran up the crater.

Lightning bolts hammered the ground.

Jerico leapt to one side.

Then another.

Then another.

Lightning bolts were everywhere.

Immense chunks of mountain rock fell down around him.

Jerico ran away from the crater.

The chunks of rock hammered the ground.

And then Jerico went down the crater as fast as he could but he already knew it was way, way too late to save anyone.

As the storm screamed a final time and unleashed vast amounts of magical energy into the atmosphere that scorched Jerico's lungs and made him scream out in agony, Jerico collapsed to his knees as he saw what the hell had happened.

All the Soul Stones were gone now and where they had once been was littered with the corpses of humans and Keres alike. A lot of the rock inside the crater was charred and smouldering so Jerico had no idea what had caused that.

But he had failed.

It was Jerico's job to protect his men, protect the Keres and make sure that whatever had happened today was going to happen without a single problem.

He was nothing but a failure.

Jerico had no idea how he was going to contact the families, friends and loved ones of his proud wonderful men that had died under his command. He couldn't tell the families any of the details because it was illegal for humans to work with the Keres but he wanted to help the victims of this attack somehow.

Jerico saw something move below him.

Jerico slowly went down into the crater with his machine gun ready to fire if needed. The entire crater smelt awful of charred flesh, burnt ozone and another strange burnt smell that was probably to do with the sheer amount of magic in the air.

"You live," a female Keres said in her blood soaked and blackened robes.

Jerico rushed over to her and held her in his arms. He applied pressure to the wound but it was still flowing too quickly. She was going to die and it would be all his fault.

"I'm sorry I failed," Jerico said.

The woman laughed. "You did not fail Son of Genetrix. This outcome was already predetermined by the Goddess and this has the potential to save or doom all life in the galaxy,"

"I don't understand,"

"Humans never do," the woman said. "The Goddess works in magical ways. She came to me with the last of her power a century ago so I could find the Soulstones and Rebirth her so she may walk amongst the stars like she did millions of years ago,"

"But I failed you," Jerico said.

"This is not the right time for Genetrix to return," the woman said. "And now know that I was not the one to Rebirth her. There is a human woman called Ithane Veilwalker, she is the true Daughter of Genetrix,"

Jerico wasn't sure. Why the hell would a Keres Goddess want to have a mere human as her chosen.

"You must find her, protect her and keep her safe. She has just been reborn herself and you must find her. It is only through her that Geneitor is defeated and life in the galaxy will continue. Will you do that for me?"

Jerico nodded because he flat out hated the feeling of her warm blood oozing all over his hands as he failed yet again to save her life.

"Good," the woman said grinning. "Then take my necklace too. The Goddess was clever and she showed me the way. Take the necklace and may the Soulstone of Spero, Goddess of Hope, guide you like it has me,"

Jerico was about to question it. He couldn't be entrusted with such an important task, he was a failure, he was nothing, he was a mere human. But the female Keres died in his arms and he simply took off the golden necklace with the weird blue crystal at the end of it, and smiled.

He had no idea what the future was going to offer. The future could have been dark horrid and filled with suffering for all he knew but he had his mission and he had his destiny already laid out for him.

He wasn't sure that any human truly understood what intergalactic and maybe even interdimensional game of God and Goddess they were all blindly entering into, but that didn't matter. Because he was going to find this Ithane woman, he was going to find the Soulstones once more and he was going to succeed this time.

And bring down Geneitor once and for all.

All because he had hope for a better future, a better life and hopefully redemption for allowing all the amazing people around him to die, when they really didn't need to.

DARK MEALS

The icy cold dark void of space had always comforted Lady Anna of the House of The Deadly Rose, she had always loved how the dark tendrils of space seek to reach out and wrap around the innocent circular ships that dared to travel through it all, and that was why Anna only ever dared to hold court in space.

Some people believed that the Noble Houses were mere relics of a bygone age and everyone was just waiting until the Rex finally gave the most holy order to exterminate them all. Since technically and according to Imperial Law that even the Rex hadn't dare touched himself, it was only the Noble Houses that could become Emperor or Empress of the Imperium.

And that was Anna's endgame.

She sat on at the head of a dark blood-red metal table that she only ever bought out for these sort of special occasions. It was a beautiful handcrafted artisan piece her mother had collected over two hundred years old on some radioactive wasteland of a planet, but Anna still loved it.

The table had such impressive, curved lines that always made the eye want to follow the natural curves of the table to see the other guests sitting at the table. Anna supposed it was an engineering marvel that the sheer elegance of the table made it impossible to avoid conversation between guests.

Her favourite piece of the stunning table probably had to be the strange lumpy yet smooth texture of the table. It looked so rough, lumpy and interesting with its blood-red surface being covered in tiny shards of bones (human bones to be exact) but whenever she ran her fingers over its cold surface she was surprised how smooth it was.

The entire oval chamber of the black circular warship was filled with the delightful aromas of crispy roasted hog, fatty, juicy, succulent pulled pork and a rainbow of vegetables from so many different planets that Anna had no intention of explaining all the origins to her guests.

They would all be dead soon anyway.

Anna had made sure that the three crystal bowls filled with blue, pink and orange tomatoes were sliced perfectly and arranged in such a stunning way that the bowl looked like it had baby swans inside.

She was so glad she had hired that celebrity chef before he was executed for treason on that mining world.

The gentle hum of the engines made Anna just smile as the large circular doors to the chamber opened and her five guests walked in. The gentleness of the hum was a weird reminder of that as far as her guests were concerned they were going to leave this meeting a very rich group of Imperial Governors.

In reality they were all going to die.

Anna didn't want to kill them all but to keep her family, friends and her way of life safe she was going to have to. And the least she could do was have fun doing it.

She was disappointed that all five of the governors (three men and two women) all wore the exact same boring imperial governor uniform. The pig ugly black soldier uniform with the golden metal symbol of the Rex over the chest plate and the stripes and crowns of their position wielded strongly onto their armour.

Their metal boots pounded the freshly polished marble floor, Anna was definitely going to kill them if they dared chip her floor, and they all took a seat at the dinner.

Interestingly a very tall and heavily armoured woman with long fiery hair sat at the opposite end of the table. Anna couldn't understand why this woman thought she was another head of the table but Anna was more than willing to show her her mistake.

"How do you plan to kill us then?" the fiery

woman asked.

Anna smiled.

Of course she had always expected that Imperial Governors were intelligent. They had to be to avoid upsetting the Rex, being killed and erased from the official records but Anna had no idea they knew about her plan to kill them.

She had poisoned their food naturally with a slow-acting poison that couldn't be treated but she had managed to micro-dose herself enough over the past few years so she was immune to its effects.

And yet she couldn't understand how these people knew about her plan. She had told her small staff but that was it and the staff were way too loyal to her to betray her. In fact they all knew Anna was doing this treacherous plan to help them.

She was being selfless here.

"I was thinking about poisoning your food," Anna said, "but I am more interested in knowing how you knew I planned to kill you all,"

Everyone else except the woman with the fiery hair frowned.

"We know the Noble Houses are planning to kill the Rex," the woman said. "My name is Lady Ella of the House of the Death Flower,"

Anna smiled. It was always nice to be in the presence of another Noble House member but that particular house was destroyed decades ago when the Rex wanted to show the Noble Houses that he and only he was in charge of the Imperium.

Anna had sadly lost way too many friends in that purge so how did Ella survive?

"The Noble Houses can work with the Rex," Ella said. "My House refused to work with him but I did, and now look at me I have the power and influence and-"

"And the stupidity to believe he cares about you," Anna said. "The Rex has already destroyed humanity from the peaceful race that we once were. It is only a matter of time until you have outlived your usefulness and then he will kill you,"

Anna noticed the other four people sitting at the table were staring at the silver palates of meat, sliced sausages and more delights with large hungry eyes.

"You can eat it," Anna said.

Ella stood up and took out a small gun-like device and she scanned the table using it.

Anna bit her lip as she suspected it was a poison neutraliser. She had no clue how they worked but she had read a lot about them recently. They effectively made her poison useless.

Then everyone started eating the cold and hot meats, the crispy vegetables and the thick creamy sauces.

"We came here because we know you are a traitor to the Rex," Ella said taking a slice of Hog tongue, "so after this meal you will be executed and your crew will be enslaved,"

Anna laughed. She absolutely couldn't allow that,

she knew she was done for but she couldn't allow anything to happen to her friends and her crew and she would have to attempt to save her family on their homeworld somehow.

She was screwed.

Anna looked at the amazing food that had been grown on so many planets that this single table probably represented all the Farming Worlds in the Imperium. She had to survive.

"How would you kill us now?" one of the men asked chomping on a Hog leg the size of his arm.

Anna cocked her head. That was a good question. "I would order my soldiers to kill you but I suspect they're unavailable,"

Ella nodded. "Of course they are. We tasered them all on the way to you and that's why even if you scream there will be no guards to save you,"

Anna had to admit that was damn well annoying.

"It was your relationship with Lord Iron of the House of The Fist that really doomed you," Ella said.

Anna didn't want to even admit that any sort of relationship had happened. It was a fling, a bunch of cheap meaningless hook-ups and the best sex she had ever had. At least that was what she kept telling herself after he had defected to the Enlightened Republic.

The amazingly brave and brilliant solar systems that wanted to live in a fair, free and democratic society that was the polar opposite of the Imperium. He had wanted her to go but Anna was just too much of a coward.

Now she really wished she had left with him. The man she probably could have fallen for in the end.

"This meat is delicious. I don't know how you got it from the Deathly Halls but I'm glad you did," another man said as he stuffed his face full of dark, crispy fried meat that crunched loudly.

Anna smiled because it was nice that the others respected her choice of food and her influence to actually get it all here but maybe that was her salvation.

If she could prove she was useful to these folks then maybe Ella wouldn't kill her or maybe, just maybe the others wouldn't let Ella kill her.

"I'm sure my supplier would love to give you all a good sampling of his products but it's a shame he only deals with me," Anna said.

In truth it was a female trader that helped her gather up all these meats and exotic vegetables both inside and outside official channels but the others did not need to know that.

The man stuffing his face had longish brown hair that made him rather attractive in a bad boy sort of way but Anna just wanted to manipulate him right now.

"That's right," Anna said. "The meat sounds good, doesn't it? Nice and fatty and thick with power. I'm you know all about that,"

The man blushed and everyone except Ella

laughed hard.

"You need to watch your back traitor," Ella said. "The only reason why you are still alive is because we wanted to know what your plan was but you are clearly too stupid for that,"

Anna stood up and chomped on a rich, oily, perfectly seasoned slice of juicy tomato.

"I might not be involved in the plots you think I am but I am still the master of my ship and I do intend to kill you all but I am a Noblewoman first and foremost. So how about a transaction?"

Ella shook her head but the others leant forward. Ella clearly wasn't as powerful as she believed.

"What sort of transaction?" the face-stuffing man asked.

"My life for all the rich tasty meats and vegetables you desire," Anna said.

It might have sounded lame but this was all about control and the Rex was a master of it. It was a well-known fact that the Rex always made sure to give enough food and drink to a given planet to make sure the population didn't starve to death.

But he also made sure not to give them too much so the population was still docile and needy. The same rules applied for governors and other planetary officials unless you lived on Earth so it was little wonder why these governors were so interested in a few extra food.

It also helped that all these meats were extremely high in tasty fats so if anything changed the governors would have a store of fat in them to buy them a few extra weeks.

Food was a method of control in the Imperium.

Ella whipped out a gun.

Anna sat down and the other men and women looked at each other. They were clearly considering their options.

Anna normally had a gun on her but she hadn't needed it tonight so far because the poison would have been enough to kill them. She really wished she had a gun now.

"Lady Anna in the name of the Rex you are a traitor!" Ella shouted. "And your life is forfeit!"

Anna smiled as Ella fired.

Someone flapped their arms about.

The laser blast flashed in front of her but nothing hit her and then Anna saw the thin shimmer of a shield in front of her and the other governors at the table were smiling.

It was standard for governors to carry all sorts of strange and wonderful equipment with them just in case they were ever in danger. And thankfully that always included a small shield generator.

So at least the arm flapping now made sense as it was someone throwing the tiny generator in her direction.

Anna stood up and went straight over to Ella.

Ella looked so weakened, surprised and terrified and she honestly had every right to be.

Anna snatched the gun out of her hand and she pressed it against Ella's forehead.

Ella was about to speak but Anna fired and milliseconds later boiling brain matter splashed over the floor away from the table. She wasn't going to spoil the food for any reason.

Ella's corpse landed with a thud and Anna simply went back to her seat at the head of the table and she spoke calmly, collectively and hopefully with each of the other governors at the table.

Because she had found allies and she was finally going to live.

***

A month later, Anna sat back in the dining chamber with the beautiful blood-red table under her as she was sitting on the table for a change and she just stared out the massive floor-to-ceiling windows just watching space streak past her.

After the great night with the governors, they had all paid her excessive amounts of money and she had placed orders for them and their planets to get them exclusive meats and drinks that would help their populations thrive for another few years. More than enough time for them to plan how they would rebel against the Rex.

And that was certainly something that Anna was surprised about, at the end of the night there seemed to be such a fierce conviction in the eyes of the governors that they really, really didn't want to play the Rex's game anymore.

A game of death, oppression and ultimately enslavement. Humanity was dying because of the Rex so Anna understood why they wanted out and she was fully intending to help them.

In a few minutes she would be in the Enlightened Republic and then she would hopefully find the man she loved, get involved in the Republic and then the fight to save humanity would well and truly begin.

Anna had bought all her friends, her family and her crew along because she had to protect them no matter the cost and that was exactly what she was doing. Taking them from a dangerous, unloving Imperium to somewhere that offered hope, love and a chance of freedom.

As the engines hummed as they exited Ultraspace, Anna grinned as she saw the stunning Republic and she knew, just knew that this was where she was meant to be. She was safe, at home and she had finally found her purpose.

A purpose to help free humanity and stop the tyranny of the Rex once and for all.

DEATH OF A FAMILIAR

Today taught me why humans couldn't be trusted because this was the day I died for my Goddess.

The last thing I would ever call humans is normal. They are strange, complex and very smelly creatures with their soft flesh, large waists and they are just weird to look at.

I had met many humans over my long life on many worlds that I mostly forget now, but the story of humanity and their species is all the same. War, killing and blind ignorance of the truth about the universe.

And I should know to be honest because as I curl up in my wonderfully soft purple Familiar bed, that a bastard human had once decided to call a "cat bed" as if I was such a low life as a cat. I was a Familiar of the Keres race, a cat-like creature with much more beautiful, softer and striking purple fur given life by the Goddess Genetrix herself. I was not a cat.

But yet I digress, my apologies.

You see I was all nice and toasty and curled up on my bed, allowing the wonderful warmth that my magic pulsed into the velvet fabric, to travel back into me. It was like sitting on a warm metal chair without the intensity of the heat. I loved it.

I rested my little head on the edge of the bed and stared out at my boss's new room that was oddly human and I hated it. considering my boss was a Keres, a much thinner, pure and magical version of humanity created by the Goddess of Life Genetrix millions of years ago, I didn't understand the human decorations.

The office itself was a massive grey metal box in my opinion with weird orbs of bright white golden light floating near the dark grey ceiling. The little orbs were pretty to look at as they bounced along the ceiling causing shadows to dance across the grey floor.

The entire office just looked cold and isolated and not Keres at all. I had always loved the wonderfully dark purple, red and blue crystals that the Keres manipulated to create whatever their impressive minds could develop. By contrast human design just always felt a little lacking.

My boss was sitting at her ugly massive desk that was an immense slab of grey metal with some cute Keres items on them. I noticed she had a glass bowl of blue glowing crystals that she had placed a magical shield over to stop me devouring all those delicious treats at once.

She was crafty like that.

But I could sense my boss was tense, nervous and her single claw tapped loudly against the metal desk.

She had developed that clawed finger way before I was gifted to her by the Goddess but it had apparently happened during a spell gone wrong. She had wanted to cast a torrent of fire at some humans that were going to kill some innocent people but the spell backfired.

She tried to focus too much magic through a single finger so the finger exploded, killed the humans and saved the innocent but the finger had twisted into a claw.

A cold, dead, awful-looking claw.

"Do you sense the humans yet?" my boss asked me.

I wasn't even sure why my boss wanted to see a whole bunch of smelly humans today in this awful office. Even the hints of human coffee, caramel and toffee that stunk out the air was out of place and I might have been lending my magic to create the smell but it was still out of place.

The only benefit was the great taste of toffee that formed on my tongue. I did enjoy it when humans brought me treats like that.

"Tazzie," my boss said, "do you sense the

humans?"

I closed my eyes briefly and coursed my magic through the immense crystal-like ship we were currently on. The banging, humming and popping of the ship tried to interfere with my senses but it failed.

I felt the darkness of the Death God Geneitor press against my mind but I couldn't allow the Great Enemy to stop me. I coursed my magic through the entire ship and then I detected the dull glow of human souls boarding.

"Of course," I said almost offended my boss actually believed I wouldn't be able to. "I still do not understand the importance of seeing the humans in *this* place,"

My boss stood up and I admired her long blond golden hair that framed her sharp, pointed face and ears perfectly.

"These humans are not from the Imperium and they do not serve the Rex. They could be allies in the fight to save the Keres,"

I didn't bother moving my head because I was comfortable and enjoying the warmth far too much to risk moving. But I still rolled my eyes.

I really did like my boss and I was grateful for the Goddess to gift me to her, but she was an idiot at times. The tyrannical awful Imperium and that monstrous Rex, their leader, would hunt down every single element of the Keres they couldn't manipulate or control. And then one day they would want to wipe us all out.

It was simply the truth.

The Death God wanted to obliterate Genetrix's creations and he was using humanity to do it. Yet because humanity refused to believe in the simple truth that the two divine beings existed, they were walking themselves further and further into damnation with each passing day.

I doubt these humans would be any different.

"You doubt me?" my boss said.

I grinned and tried to hide my fang-like teeth from her. "Of course I doubt you. I doubt your entire race at times because of what you allowed to happen and continues to happen,"

My boss stood up perfectly straight as we both realised the humans were coming closer to the office.

"The main Keres race might be happy living by the monstrous terms of the Treaty of Defeat that means we're slaves to humanity but I will not allow that. It is why I serve the Goddess as a Daughter of Genetrix,"

I nodded and smiled as the cold metal door of the office hissed open and three humans walked in.

I covered my nose with a purple paw as the foul aroma of sweat, blood and human waste filled the air. I am sure they wouldn't have smelt to other humans but I was a Familiar and my senses were extreme.

Even my boss didn't seem to notice too much.

Boss clicked her fingers and three very human wooden chairs appeared. I was disgusted in how simple and artless the humans were about their chairs. It was a crime against the beauty that Genetrix placed in the world but I had to behave.

"Who is the cat?" one of the humans asked but at this point they all looked as weird as each other.

"Tazzie is not a cat. She is a Familiar gifted to me by Genetrix, Creator of Life,"

I rolled my eyes and leapt from my bed to the desk making all the humans jump.

I stood there as Boss continued to introduce the mission of the Daughter of Genetrix and how they wanted to protect both the Keres and humanity from the predations of Geneitor.

I rolled my eyes again at the humans but they were all wearing bright baby blue military uniforms and I could sense there was darkness in each of them. It wasn't a massive amount of darkness or even something to be alarmed about, but something wasn't right.

"Why is the Familiar looking at us?" the human to my left asked.

"Her job is threefold. She is meant to protect me, amplify my power and serve Genetrix however she sees fit," Boss said.

I stared at the human. "And sometimes that means killing whoever attacks us,"

The humans smiled like I was some type of domestic play animal that couldn't possibly hurt them.

"We have been sent here by the Enlightened

Republic to support you in exchange for you helping us," the tallest human said taking out a something large wrapped in black cloth.

I hissed as soon as I sensed the darkness and Death Magic pouring out of the black cloth.

I flashed my fangs at the humans but again they didn't seem concerned at all. They were more focused on Boss as she hissed and wiped her nose like trying to wipe away a bad smell.

The human placed the object on the desk so I backed away and smiled as even the desk groaned in protest of having something so dark on it.

"So the humans bring us a Death Object," I said through clenched teeth. That had to be a foul crime itself and it was outrageous that the humans had discovered such an object in the first place.

No wonder I had sensed Darkness in them. The mere exposure to such an object would cause Geneitor's influence to take root in their mind, body and soul.

"This is outrageous, Boss," I said. "The Goddess would never allow this object on one of her ships,"

Without warning the humans took off the black cloth and they made sure a small piece of the cloth touched my paw.

The cloth burned my paw and turned the purple fur to ash. I shot backwards hissing in agony.

The air crackled with purple magical energy around me but Boss raised a warning finger at the humans and I knew she would deal with the situation.

Yet I understood why she hadn't killed the humans for now because if there was a Death Object in play then we had to deal with it and find out if the humans were a real threat or not.

I slowly went over to the bowl-like object that had been covered by the cloth and I flat out hated the weird shrieking sound that echoed inside my head. I knew the damn humans wouldn't have been able to hear it, but then again me and Boss were sensitive to this stuff.

In fact every single Keres on the ship was probably hearing this and having the Darkness try to influence and push into their minds, bodies and souls.

I didn't want to have this aboard any longer than needed but there was something weird about the design.

This particular Death Object was a large black bowl made from a strange type of glassy stone with millions of lines of writing. It was clearly Keres writing from the shape but the little black tendrils coming off the bowl made it hard to read.

I wasn't sure if those tendrils were natural or if the Goddess was trying to protect us from the evil writing.

"What is a Death Object?" a human asked.

"The stupidity of humans never ceases to amaze me. It is amazing you primitives can even begin to understand the grandeur of the universe," I said flicking my two tails harshly.

"Come, come now Tazzie. The humans are silly in their beliefs for sure but there is power in their ignorance. They are likely to be corrupted by the Death magic which this bowl serves as a container,"

"The question is what do the humans want us to help them with?" I asked staring at the tallest of the humans.

The humans grinned. "We need you to help us destroy it because it is making a madness spread over an entire world in the Republic,"

I gave Boss a sideways glance. It wasn't unheard of to hear about such an event happening, and I know there had been plenty of victims of Death Magic over the past tens of thousands of years.

But no humans or even Keres could touch a Death Object without falling under its corrupting power.

Boss held her hand over the surface of the bowl and bright white magic crackled in the air and I lent her some of my strength.

I could sense her magic trying to tap into the Darkness to study it, see what could happen and to see if there was a spirit we could fight.

But this was a unique Death Object that made the foul aroma of charred flesh, hair and death fill my senses.

"How did the humans touch this without fall to the Darkness?" I asked knowing it was impossible.

The humans looked nervously at each other. "We made a deal with a man that appeared when we touched the bowl,"

I prepared to pounce and Boss magicked a long purple sword out of thin air.

The humans grinned and they spoke as one. "It was a good deal for humanity. They sold their souls to me and in exchange I allow them to take the bowl off-world,"

Boss shook her head and I sensed her psychically battling with the Death creature that had clearly possessed the poor stupid humans.

The humans took a few steps back and I watched the humans and Boss stare into each other's eyes. There was clearly going to be as much a war of words here as much a psychic battle I was going to help with at some point.

"Why allow them to take the Bowl off-world?" Boss asked focusing on the humans intensely. "It makes no sense because you could corrupt millions of souls so why settle for three?"

"Because the humans would come here," I said staring at the bowl as the dark tendrils started to shrink back. Probably because the Death Creature had to use their magic in the mental battle with Boss instead of using it to protect the bowl.

That meant it was weaker.

Boss screamed out in pain and gripped her head as the Creature striked a mental blow.

I lent Boss all the strength I could.

Boss thrusted out her hand. Flattening a human

against a wall. Bones cracked and organs exploded painting the walls of the office in dark red blood.

The other two humans laughed as their skin turned deathly black and their veins glowed sickly yellow.

The humans charged into each other and became one twisted, deformed walking corpse that made the air crackle with black magical energy.

"Death Creatures I hate them," I said my tails flickering around wildly.

I hissed as loud as I could sending the magical soundwaves slamming into the Creature.

Boss flew at the Creature. I had to do my part. I couldn't fight it. I still had to help Boss.

I spun around and focused on the evil Bowl. It was glowing dark evil black and I could sense the Darkness start to take root in the hull of the ship.

That had been the bastard's plan the entire time. Keres souls were brighter, purer and so-called tastier than human souls. So Geneitor planned to corrupt the ship inside out so he could force an entire ship's worth of Daughter of Genetrix to fall to his worship.

It was monstrous, pure monstrous.

I raised a paw. My claws shot out. I striked the Bowl.

Crippling pain filled me. My bones moved violently and I felt like my paw would shatter.

The Bowl hissed in pain as I realised how weak and helpless the Bowl was. It wasn't made from stone it was made from the dreams and delusions of the

Death Creature.

It wasn't real. It was an abomination on the Goddess's work.

I clawed it again.

A massive chunk of it turned to ash but I was in agony. I was in so much crippling pain that I couldn't hiss or meow or do anything.

I tried to raise my claws again but I couldn't. I was in too much pain.

Boss screamed.

I spun around. Sending two fireballs at the Death Creature allowing Boss to jump up and slash at his chest a little.

Pure magical energy filled me from the Goddess because I had to do this, I had to annihilate the bowl despite the pain but I couldn't.

But I had to do my duty.

I struck the bowl but my paw collapsed into the bowl like it had been eaten and all the pain receptors had been consumed.

I just looked down at my poor little paw as it was no longer there and I felt the corrupting influence of the Darkness pulse up my arm and my heartbeat flooded my body with the corrupted blood.

I felt the warmth and wonderful life that the Goddess filled me with start to become more distant as her power was fading from me.

Boss screamed as she realised I was dying and the Death Creature laughed.

I screamed in defiance and charged at the Bowl. The dark tendrils shot back in fear and I smashed into it with such force it flew off the desk.

Smashing onto the ground below. Turning to ash.

The Creature hissed and screamed out in a deafening roar as it started to dissolve because it couldn't remain in reality without an anchor. Something I had just annihilated.

As the threat was dead, the humans were no more and the ship was saved from Geneitor's corruption, I collapsed to the ground as my paws and body were slowly devoured by the corrupting Darkness that had taken root within me.

"At least Genetrix will grab my soul before Geneitor can torture it forever," I said trying to smile but accidentally flashing my fangs.

I could see how badly Boss wanted to touch me, cuddle me and stroke my blackening fur a final time. I would have loved that too but she couldn't become corrupted herself because the ship needed her, the Daughters of Genetrix needed her and most importantly the Goddess needed every able servant ready for the war to come.

Geneitor was growing stronger and stronger and if he reached full strength then he would happily devour all life in the galaxy and then the universe.

Something none of us could allow.

"I love you," I said to Boss. "You're a good woman, a good fighter and hell of a Servant of the

Goddess,"

She smiled and I noticed a small crystal tear start to form in her eyes and she went to say something else.

But as the Darkness continued to dissolve my body and ears, I never heard the words but I knew they were words of thanks, appreciation and love. Because I might have been difficult at times but we were Familiar and Boss, a match made in the heavens and a bond that couldn't be broken because it was stronger than love and I really did love Boss.

And I was more than happy to have died to save her, the Keres and all the innocent people they would go on to save in the name of Genetrix, Goddess, Creator and Protector of life.

DYING IN SPACE

No fuel. No power. No environmental systems.

Well, this was a massive clusterfuck if there was ever was one, and I mean I have been in some serious scraps at times. From me escaping Justices before they killed me for crimes I didn't commit, me having to escape from brainwashing camps because the so-called Rex didn't believe I was worshipping him enough and me having to stitch up my infected laser wounds from stupid Imperial Soldiers shooting at me.

I was very well known to pain, agony and annoying people unfortunately.

But even I have to admit that this might actually be my final trip in the Imperium because I sit on the icy cold black metal floor of my bridge, just a posh name for a small circular disc on top of my circular shuttle with a few ugly grey consoles and a broken metal throne on it. That throne was meant to be where I commanded the shuttle from but it was broken.

So the controls were broken.

Three bright flashes lit up the void in the

distance.

I'd been on this damn shuttle for days now, cruising past bright fiery white stars that shone like mocking beacons of hope as my misery only grew, and now I was well and truly fucked.

I was nothing more than a mere floating shard of metal flying through the pitch darkness of space without any planets, help or humans nearby.

Part of me wondered if I actually would have liked some company, I hated the idea of dying alone and forgotten but I suppose that's just my large human ego that pops up from time to time. And true to behold, having other people here might just get me killed, so I had to be alone.

The silence of the shuttle was deafening and I seriously wasn't a fan of the silence. For the past few months I had been listening to the constant hum, pop and bang of various systems keeping the shuttle working perfectly, so the silence was just creepy.

Even the air was strange now with its delightfully sweet aromas of basil, tomatoes and garlic from my dinners being replaced with burnt oil and burnt flesh. I really didn't want to know what on Earth had been cooked in the engines.

Three huge flashes appeared at the corner of my eye.

My engines were completely dead, my environmental systems weren't recycling oxygen anymore and even the emergency power of the ship wasn't working.

Thankfully I somehow had some anti-gravity left over but even that seemed to be failing slowly so I was seriously running out of time to somehow get rescued. Or I would die.

I supposed I could have called in Imperial Rescue but even though they pretended to be an independent organisation from the Rex and his Imperial Government, everyone knew they were working for him directly. As soon as I notified them, they would send warships to my location and I would be slaughtered.

You might be wondering what I possibly could have done to piss off the Imperium so much?

And I will most certainly tell you my good man (or woman), I simply questioned the Imperium. You see ever since humanity crawled out of the oceans, developed limbs to become apes and then evolve into humans, they have always learnt.

I wanted to learn about the wider galaxy so I studied astrophysics at the University of Earth, one of the top universities in the Imperium but it was also one of the most censored by the Rex.

A lot of my classmates didn't realise that whilst our lectures, assignments and textbooks were long, they were very skilfully crafted to make us *seem* like we were learning tons but we actually weren't. We weren't being taught anything that the Rex perceived to be forbidden knowledge and the Rex loved people to believe that all knowledge was bad knowledge.

In reality if humanity was dumb then it made them a lot more compliant with whatever he wanted to do.

So I setup out to learn more about the galaxy, the Rex found out and now he was hunting me because I had learnt more about the galaxy in two weeks than I had learnt in four years of my undergraduate degree. That was how controlling the Rex was.

A flash appeared outside.

I stood up and forced my breathing to remain level as I was very conscious about the lack of oxygen in the bridge and I didn't dare waste a single gram of it. I really wanted to be saved but this was a very dodgy part of the Imperium.

I peered out into the pitch darkness of space and whilst there were no planets nearby I did notice a large black cube outside.

The cube itself was pitch black, perfectly smooth and about the size of a human's head. I could only see it because of the reflection off a distant star.

I wanted to reach out and touch it but I couldn't because of my bridge's windows and I knew it was most probably dangerous.

One cube became three cubes.

I had backed away from the windows and I just shook my head in disbelief. I had no idea where the other two cubes came from but this was serious now.

Metal cubes didn't just appear out of nowhere and given how I was still in the Imperium I was willing to bet that these were sensory drones belonging to pirates, aliens or the Imperium.

Pirates would simply smash up my ship and make me a slave. The foul alien Keres would probably savage my ship and use their corrupting magic to turn me into a mindless drone for them. The Imperium would simply kill me.

I was screwed whatever happened.

I felt a wave pass through me and the black cubes started to slowly tap on the glass.

Shit. This was exactly what I didn't want. These cubes had to be testing how to get to me and then kill me.

I looked around the bridge and thankfully I had stolen two brand-new environmental suits from the last owners of this shuttle so I went over to the back of the bridge.

I slowly removed a large grey panel in the smooth walls and I smiled at the two bright red environmental suits. A loud high-pitched buzz echoed around me making me jump.

The black cubes were glowing red at me and I couldn't help but feel like the cubes were trying to warn me against putting on the suit.

To hell with them. They were going to kill me anyway so I might as well make the job a little bit harder for them.

I took out the two suits and each one had a small metal backpack on them with all the oxygen recyclers and air filters inside so I decided to disconnect one backpack on one suit and connect it to the other suit.

I had heard rumours of people using two backpacks before and it worked fine. Hell the suits were actually designed for three air-filtering backpacks but budget cuts made them reduce the number down to one.

The high-pitch scream got even louder and I stopped dead in my tracks.

I heard the deafening sound of glass cracking around me.

I couldn't waste any more time so I got the environmental suit on as quickly as possible and I activated the backpack.

Choking green gas filled my environment suit. I shut off the power but it was too late.

I ripped off my helmet and collapse to the ground as the choking green gas filtered out into the bridge and I felt my lungs burn in agony.

My vision blurred for a few moments and I seriously hated everything that was happening to me.

My eyes were so watery that I only heard the smashing of the windows but oddly enough no air rushed out and I wasn't sucked out into space.

I just sat there with my lungs burning up and I could have saw I felt icy cold liquid start to fill them. I had heard plenty of times about dry drowning and how toxic gas made the lungs drown themselves.

I just hadn't ever wanted it to happen to me.

I rolled over onto my back and rolled my eyes as

I watched the three little cubes hover around me like bees inspecting a new plant to devour but the sound was unreal. Each of the cubes were singing a soothing melody and relaxed me, made me happy and made me very, very sleepy.

I fought to stay awake and the crippling pain filled my senses was overwhelming and I didn't want to fall asleep as my lungs filled with oxygen.

I coughed loudly enough to drown out the sweet melody of the cubes but they only got louder and within seconds my world collapsed around me.

***

"He should be waking up… now,"

My eyes snapped open and I gasped at the absolutely beautiful woman in front of me. The woman standing over me had long sexy blond hair, a radiant smile and a shockingly stunning face that was angles and lines.

She might have been wearing a long innocent white dress but that also made me perfectly aware that I was naked and I wasn't even on a bed.

I looked around at a very beautiful large white domed room I was in. It had to be some kind of hospital room but instead of the undertone of death, destruction and harsh cleaning chemicals I had known from watching my mother die in the Imperium. This hospital room smelt delightful of flowers.

The sound of people laughing, singing and talking about sports outside my room made me smile because this sure as hell wasn't the Imperium, so maybe I had died and gone to where dead people go after death.

The woman smiled at me and sadly stepped away from me so I was blinded by a bright beautiful sun and a large crystal clear blue sky that stretched on endlessly through a domed window. I wasn't on the first floor but I was amazed at the sheer scale of the breath-taking domed city I was in.

"Welcome to the Enlightened Republic Hayden," the woman said.

I had no idea how the woman knew my name but I was glad she did.

"I am Supreme General Abbie of the Enlightened Republic so I'm in charge of greeting the new arrivals from the Imperium," she said.

I just smiled. I had heard so many rumours of the Enlighted Republic and it just seemed impossible to believe that it was actually real and not some strange figure of humanity's imagination.

A republic that believed in hope, democracy and freedom. Three ideals that formed the great core of this Republic but I knew they were alien concepts to the Imperium.

"I have a lot to learn don't I?" I asked.

Abbie laughed beautifully and nodded. "Of course you do but so do so many others. We have thousands of drones all over the Imperium watching for anyone approaching us in case they want to kill us, but we also use them to know when someone needs help,"

I could only nod I was so glad that the cubes were friends, not foes.

"The sweet melody was designed by my daughter working on brain frequency and brain activity to help an injured person fall to sleep before we teleported them back here for treatment,"

"Thank you and, what happens to me now?" I asked.

Abbie gave me a very warm smile and she gestured I go over to the domed window so I did. The window was large but the view outside was simply stunning.

For as far as I could see there were people happy, singing and dancing in the wide open streets with a thriving market below selling all sorts of things. Of course some people were rushing to work and others were couples kissing in the street.

And that was a hell of a culture shock. People could never kiss in public, sell goods outside of Rex-approved channels and they certainly couldn't dance in the street.

"This is the future," Abbie said.

I could only smile as I realised that she was right. The Enlightened Republic was a hell of a future because I would finally be free and that really was the most precious thing of all and I was looking forward to exploring, helping and living in this wonderfully new world that had yet to be explored by me.

WAY OF THE ODYSSEY SHORT STORY COLLECTION VOLUME 3

GET YOUR FREE SHORT STORY NOW!

And get signed up to Connor Whiteley's newsletter to hear about new gripping books, offers and exciting projects. (You'll never be sent spam)

https://www.subscribepage.io/garrosignup

About the author:

Connor Whiteley is the author of over 60 books in the sci-fi fantasy, nonfiction psychology and books for writer's genre and he is a Human Branding Speaker and Consultant.

He is a passionate warhammer 40,000 reader, psychology student and author.

Who narrates his own audiobooks and he hosts The Psychology World Podcast.

All whilst studying Psychology at the University of Kent, England.

Also, he was a former Explorer Scout where he gave a speech to the Maltese President in August 2018 and he attended Prince Charles' 70th Birthday Party at Buckingham Palace in May 2018.

Plus, he is a self-confessed coffee lover!

WAY OF THE ODYSSEY SHORT STORY COLLECTION VOLUME 3

<u>Other books by Connor Whiteley:</u>

<u>Bettie English Private Eye Series</u>
A Very Private Woman
The Russian Case
A Very Urgent Matter
A Case Most Personal
Trains, Scots and Private Eyes
The Federation Protects
Cops, Robbers and Private Eyes
Just Ask Bettie English
An Inheritance To Die For
The Death of Graham Adams
Bearing Witness
The Twelve
The Wrong Body
The Assassination Of Bettie English
Wining And Dying
Eight Hours
Uniformed Cabal
A Case Most Christmas

<u>Gay Romance Novellas</u>
Breaking, Nursing, Repairing A Broken Heart
Jacob And Daniel
Fallen For A Lie
Spying And Weddings
Clean Break

Awakening Love
Meeting A Country Man
Loving Prime Minister
Snowed In Love
Never Been Kissed
Love Betrays You

<u>Lord of War Origin Trilogy:</u>
Not Scared Of The Dark
Madness
Burn Them All

<u>The Fireheart Fantasy Series</u>
Heart of Fire
Heart of Lies
Heart of Prophecy
Heart of Bones
Heart of Fate

<u>City of Assassins (Urban Fantasy)</u>
City of Death
City of Marytrs
City of Pleasure
City of Power

WAY OF THE ODYSSEY SHORT STORY
COLLECTION VOLUME 3

<u>Agents of The Emperor</u>
Return of The Ancient Ones
Vigilance
Angels of Fire
Kingmaker
The Eight
The Lost Generation
Hunt
Emperor's Council
Speaker of Treachery
Birth Of The Empire
Terraforma
Spaceguard

<u>The Rising Augusta Fantasy Adventure Series</u>
Rise To Power
Rising Walls
Rising Force
Rising Realm

<u>Lord Of War Trilogy (Agents of The Emperor)</u>
Not Scared Of The Dark
Madness
Burn It All Down

Miscellaneous:
RETURN
FREEDOM
SALVATION
Reflection of Mount Flame
The Masked One
The Great Deer
English Independence

OTHER SHORT STORIES BY CONNOR WHITELEY

<ins>Mystery Short Story Collections</ins>
Criminally Good Stories Volume 1: 20 Detective Mystery Short Stories
Criminally Good Stories Volume 2: 20 Private Investigator Short Stories
Criminally Good Stories Volume 3: 20 Crime Fiction Short Stories
Criminally Good Stories Volume 4: 20 Science Fiction and Fantasy Mystery Short Stories
Criminally Good Stories Volume 5: 20 Romantic Suspense Short Stories

WAY OF THE ODYSSEY SHORT STORY COLLECTION VOLUME 3

<u>Mystery Short Stories:</u>
Protecting The Woman She Hated
Finding A Royal Friend
Our Woman In Paris
Corrupt Driving
A Prime Assassination
Jubilee Thief
Jubilee, Terror, Celebrations
Negative Jubilation
Ghostly Jubilation
Killing For Womenkind
A Snowy Death
Miracle Of Death
A Spy In Rome
The 12:30 To St Pancreas
A Country In Trouble
A Smokey Way To Go
A Spicy Way To GO
A Marketing Way To Go
A Missing Way To Go
A Showering Way To Go
Poison In The Candy Cane
Kendra Detective Mystery Collection Volume 1
Kendra Detective Mystery Collection Volume 2
Mystery Short Story Collection Volume 1

Mystery Short Story Collection Volume 2
Criminal Performance
Candy Detectives
Key To Birth In The Past

<u>Science Fiction Short Stories:</u>
Their Brave New World
Gummy Bear Detective
The Candy Detective
What Candies Fear
The Blurred Image
Shattered Legions
The First Rememberer
Life of A Rememberer
System of Wonder
Lifesaver
Remarkable Way She Died
The Interrogation of Annabella Stormic
Blade of The Emperor
Arbiter's Truth
Computation of Battle
Old One's Wrath
Puppets and Masters
Ship of Plague
Interrogation
Edge of Failure

WAY OF THE ODYSSEY SHORT STORY COLLECTION VOLUME 3

<u>Fantasy Short Stories:</u>
City of Snow
City of Light
City of Vengeance
Dragons, Goats and Kingdom
Smog The Pathetic Dragon
Don't Go In The Shed
The Tomato Saver
The Remarkable Way She Died
Dragon Coins
Dragon Tea
Dragon Rider

<u>All books in 'An Introductory Series':</u>
Clinical Psychology and Transgender Clients
Clinical Psychology
Careers In Psychology
Psychology of Suicide
Dementia Psychology
Clinical Psychology Reflections Volume 4
Forensic Psychology of Terrorism And Hostage-Taking
Forensic Psychology of False Allegations
Year In Psychology
CBT For Anxiety
CBT For Depression
Applied Psychology

BIOLOGICAL PSYCHOLOGY 3RD EDITION
COGNITIVE PSYCHOLOGY THIRD EDITION
SOCIAL PSYCHOLOGY- 3RD EDITION
ABNORMAL PSYCHOLOGY 3RD EDITION
PSYCHOLOGY OF RELATIONSHIPS- 3RD EDITION
DEVELOPMENTAL PSYCHOLOGY 3RD EDITION
HEALTH PSYCHOLOGY
RESEARCH IN PSYCHOLOGY
A GUIDE TO MENTAL HEALTH AND TREATMENT AROUND THE WORLD- A GLOBAL LOOK AT DEPRESSION
FORENSIC PSYCHOLOGY
THE FORENSIC PSYCHOLOGY OF THEFT, BURGLARY AND OTHER CRIMES AGAINST PROPERTY
CRIMINAL PROFILING: A FORENSIC PSYCHOLOGY GUIDE TO FBI PROFILING AND GEOGRAPHICAL AND STATISTICAL PROFILING.
CLINICAL PSYCHOLOGY
FORMULATION IN PSYCHOTHERAPY
PERSONALITY PSYCHOLOGY AND

WAY OF THE ODYSSEY SHORT STORY
COLLECTION VOLUME 3

INDIVIDUAL DIFFERENCES
CLINICAL PSYCHOLOGY REFLECTIONS VOLUME 1
CLINICAL PSYCHOLOGY REFLECTIONS VOLUME 2
Clinical Psychology Reflections Volume 3
CULT PSYCHOLOGY
Police Psychology

A Psychology Student's Guide To University
How Does University Work?
A Student's Guide To University And Learning
University Mental Health and Mindset

www.ingramcontent.com/pod-product-compliance
Lightning Source LLC
LaVergne TN
LVHW012127070526
838202LV00056B/5890